I0631758

Short
Fictional
Stories

That Could Be True

Shiela Y. Harris

ISBN-13: 978-0967931258
ISBN-10: 0967931258

Shiela Y. Harris

DEDICATION

Dedicated to everyone with an active imagination, especially to my granddaughter Ashley whose many talents encourage and inspire me

CONTENTS

Acknowledgments

Introduction

AKNOWLEDGMENTS

The gift and love of writing was inherited from my mom, Ruth L. Green and I thank God for her. One of her more endearing encouragements were her instructions for me to read and absorb everything I could because reading is powerful.

INTRODUCTION

The human mind is constantly absorbing, storing, learning and filtering so it is evident that daily life is everyday school. The make-believe can be perceived as a small gap between what reality is and what imagination is. As we intertwine the two, we can further develop and heighten our creative writing skills into a literary piece others will want to read. With this analogy, I thoroughly understand how the messes of our lives have the potential to develop into ministry or bestselling novels.

We spend time and energy trying to totally forget the negative experiences when it is far more beneficial for us to remember and then receive God's deliverance while learning from them. Divine deliverance assures as we remember the negative experiences, we are not giving the experiences consent to control how we respond or feel.

This book was a real joy to write, as I reached into and embraced my personal bag of life, extracting and mixing imagination with reality and limitless and intuitive creativity. Enjoy!

Shiela Y. Harris

Shiela Y. Harris

CHAPTER - 1

LOOKING FOR JESUS

A young woman was new in town and was searching for a church home. She prayed and asked God, with so many churches in the city how would she know which one would be right for her. God simply said, "Tell them you were invited by my Son Jesus." Sunday came and she dressed and went to the first church which was really large and the sign in front said services begin at 10:00 a.m., but the doors were locked and people were just starting to arrive at 9:55 a.m. She got out her car and was ignored because no one knew or recognized her. She stopped a member and told her she was the guest of Jesus and He is supposed to be here today. The member replied, "I don't know anyone by that name."

The next week she dressed and went to another church. Upon arrival the choir was running and rustling around in robes, children were running wildly on the parking lot unattended and women were in small groups chattering and when they saw her they snickered amongst themselves. The ushers were stationed at the front entrance and could be heard complaining and they did not notice her as she entered. She stopped and inquired, "I am a friend of Jesus and he told me He would meet me here." The usher replied, "We don't have a member with that name but you are welcome to stay for service. Here's a program, just go in and sit anywhere," (as she returned to her grumbling). After about a 10 minute wait the usher asked her to move her seat because she had sat in an unmarked reserved area. Unfortunately, the only seats left unoccupied were in the rear. The woman petitioned God in prayer again and said, "No one seems to know Jesus I cannot find Him in any church I visit." God replied, "Keep trying – you will soon find one where He abides." After a few more weeks searching she came upon a church and their sign read, "Welcome, come and worship Jesus with us!" She pulled into the parking lot and the security personnel greeted her with a smile and directed her to a parking space.

She exited her car and there were greeters lined along the way into the sanctuary smiling saying, "Welcome to our service today."

As she entered the porters greeted her with a smile and escorted her to a seat, gave her a program and walked back to their post. The lady thought, "This is a friendly place I hope Jesus is here." As she sat through the service there were a lot of things happening, video announcements about various upcoming events, emphasis on the announcements and the worship team sang for 45 minutes until the Pastor arrived. While they sang, people were walking in and out the pulpit area and the sanctuary and when the pastor arrived he received an offering. He then proceeded to acknowledge guests and emphasize other events. While the choir sang another offering was received. After sitting 90 minutes the Word was presented which lasted another 55 minutes. Then there was an altar appeal and people were prophesied to and the final offering was received. She soon realized she had been in a service for 3.5 hours and never saw Jesus.

She was beginning to become frustrated and again petitioned God because she had yet to meet Jesus. The next week she went to a service which posted their hours of service. They offered 7:00 a.m. and 9:00 a.m. Sunday morning worship services (one hour Bible Teaching on Wednesday evenings from 7:00 – 8:00 p.m.) She had arrived at 8:45 a.m. and the attendants smiled as they directed her to a parking area and asked if she had any need for assistance. They then directed her to some people who were easily identifiable because of the staff badges they wore. They had genuine smiles as greeters and they asked if she was a first time visitor. She was then escorted to a station where one could share contact information if they desired to and also received a visitor's packet of information about the ministry. As she sat in the sanctuary people seemed to be praying silently and the atmosphere was serene as if someone of great power and authority was going to be in the place. Someone approached the pulpit and asked the congregation to stand and they lead a cooperate prayer, praying for our country and its leaders, our schools, prayed for divine healing and exhorted as they declared God's presence in the service today. At 9:00 a.m. the Worship leader came to the podium and immediately began to sing songs of praise about God. Unlike the other churches she visited the leader did not prompt and prime the people; they did not testify or preachy talk between songs, they led the congregation into an awesome time of Praise. Then…the atmosphere shifted and they were asked to lift their hands (not clap) but to worship God, to talk to God. Again the leader began to sing songs to God telling Him of His goodness and greatness. Everything complemented the other (the voice of the worship leader, the voices of the team, the musicians) all were with one accord.

Nothing was too loud or harsh…it was an angelic sound a time of intimacy between her and the Father. There was such a melodious sound she began to get spiritually lost in it. There were tears rolling down the faces of the people (hers too); and the team and leader continued to exhort worship. The Pastor (who was there the entire time) came to the podium and said softly (as not to interrupt the atmosphere of worship), "Jesus is meeting us here today, lift your hands and receive Him. He's here. Just allow your spirit to rest in Him. We came that we might have a personal encounter with the Father today and He is honoring us through our worship." When all was done there had been worship for 50 minutes straight and as most of the congregants took their seats some were still saturated in an ambit of worship. To further change the atmosphere the pastor instructed the musicians to softly play, "There is none like you; no one else can touch my heart…as the praise team joined." It was an amazing experience as she sat in awe, trembling, weeping because she had experienced the glory of God.

Instead of continuing with their normal service (and as worship continued to pour out) being sensitive to the Spirit of God the pastor softly instructed us to continue with our worship as God instructed him to offer Jesus to the people because someone in the audience came to meet Jesus today. He continued gently as he stated someone came to give their life to God for the first time, some are here to be restored and some simply needing a covering. Many went to the altar, people who like her had been looking for Jesus. He prayed with those at the altar as she stood there weeping and then he dismissed the service. God's Spirit had already begun a work in those at the altar and in all in attendance. The printed program still had unfinished items but we prayed and were released.

She thanked God for the encounter and would never forget true worship.

This was not just a one-time account, it happened many times thereafter. It was truly a place where worship happened and the Spirit of Jesus reigned. When one experiences true worship, it is an experience never forgotten and always longed for.

CHAPTER - 2

THE ENTERTAINER

A young man we will call Nathan dreamed of becoming an entertainer from the time he could utter words into song. As a child he used a catsup bottle for a microphone and would sing to his audience which was plastic, miniature army men and his sister's stuffed animals. With each developing year he taught himself to dance and sing like his idols Michael Jackson, Savion Glover, Rasta Thomas, Russell Thompkins (Stylistics), Sam Cooke and Marvin Gaye.

Before Nathan was conceived and while in his mother's womb she prayed and asked God for a son. She had given birth to six beautiful daughters but how she yearned for just one son. Late one night, hours after putting her girls down for bed she prayed asking God again for a son, promising to give him back through her spiritual influence, exposure to and training him in the ways of God.

Nathan was phenomenal; he sang gospel music and had a part-time job on the weekends singing in jazz clubs. His voice was extraordinary having a unique sound and quality which seemed to be a mixture of all his musical influences. He was skilled at playing various instruments and was choreographer for the church dance ministry. Music was his life as he also recorded with other artist singing background live and in studio. When he turned twenty-one he told his mom he'd decided to take his talent into the mainstream as an entertainer. Nathan had a few auditions lined up and offers to travel with a few renowned artists. His mother shared with him how she prayed for a son and while he was yet in the womb she dedicated and promised him to God. She strongly felt he would prosper most and cause positive change in others if he would remain with the ministry of the church, but Nathan's heart and mind was set.

Sadly, not everyone in the church embraced his talent and many talked negatively about him.

Some said he was too worldly while others had no real reason to offer, they just disliked his ministry.

It was discouraging at times because he did not receive much appreciation or support from within the church. But of course, as our children will do he followed his lifelong dream traveling the direction his heart led him down the road of music. Nathan's popularity exploded overnight. For a while he continued dancing and choreographing for the church and secular scenes. He sang for mega conferences, organized a dance team that became popular in both worlds and he always kept what he did as an entertainer clean and void of sensual connotations.

While traveling the world and living what seemed to be a successful life he fathered three children but never married the mother. Nathan felt his lifestyle did not permit the time he needed to spend being a husband and a dad to his children but he was a good provider. He sent a substantial amount of money regularly, sent gifts and souvenirs from his travels, pictures and articles about his accomplishments, provided them with the latest technology in computers, tablets and cell phones and called, texted and Skype them often.

The six-week engagement came to an end and it was time to return home. Nathan talked with his family via Skype telling them about the sold-out crowds, how arduous the trip was covering sixteen cities in six-weeks, and of course how much he missed everyone. It was fun, exciting and exhausting. After powering down his tablet he thought about planning a trip for him and his kids so they could spend some quality time together then he laid down for a nap.

While traveling cross country in his own customized Forest River Berkshire, 390BH-60, $200,000 RV he was involved in an accident. The driver swerved, trying not to hit a deer, lost control and the RV went over an embankment, flipping twice before landing upright. It was a miracle no one was killed but Nathan had been thrown from the home on wheels and was badly injured. After stabilizing him and running test it was determined that he would never dance again. The disk, between the fourth and fifth vertebrae bulged profusely and required immediate surgery to relieve spinal pressure. He was in a coma for six-weeks. Prior to the accident Nathan experienced years of continued success and by the time of the accident his children were young adults. As soon as they received the tragic news they went to be by his side. While in rehab Nathan worked hard three times a day so he would walk again. As his condition improved his children broke the news to him that his mom passed away while he lay in a coma for a month, she had a massive heart attack the same night of the accident and was buried before Nathan regained consciousness.

The kids laughed and talked with their dad for what seemed hours. While enjoying his children Nathan remembers a dream or vision he had while he lay in a coma. An Angel of God appeared to him with a message that God would spare his life because there was kingdom work he still had to complete. He would still have his fame although his life would change drastically and instead of being an entertainer his life would evolve around ministry. He shared the dream with his children.

As Nathan continued rehabilitating his children had their grandmother's home refurbished and retrofitted to meet their dad's physical challenges and after his release from the hospital, Nathan moved into the home with a caregiver.

Just as God had promised, his fame continued but the life he now lived, the songs he sang, the testimony he shared no longer served as entertainment but it changed lives. He continued to travel world-wide, speaking, and singing to the glory of God. Though he has several CD projects to his credit the song most requested and that he was most remembered for was recorded by a renowned Gospel artist titled, "I Give My All to Thee."

CHAPTER - 3

POSSUM RIDGE

It's amazing that an estimated 12 million Africans were shipped as slaves to the Americas from the 16th to the 19th centuries. After years of enslavement President Abraham Lincoln freed slaves in 1863 in the southern states through the Emancipation Proclamation. Slavery was permanently abolished through the Thirteenth Amendment in December 1865.

After their freedom, many remained on the plantations as hired help or sharecroppers. There was one such place in a small town on the outskirts of Marshall, Texas called Possum Ridge. Annually around mid-summer they held a huge celebration that began with a possum hunt. Possum's are not only unpleasant looking animals but because they are nocturnal the hunt always began at midnight and ended by first light the next morning. There were games and baking contest, food prepared by the women of the town and the men barbequed pork, beef, goat and chicken. A magnificent display of fireworks lit the sky including firecrackers, rockets, sparklers; and a trophy was given to the hunter with the largest possum. Some of the freed slaves that remained in Possum Ridge worked as butlers, maids and ranch hands. John Riggers plantation home was being maintained by his widow Marian. She held bridge games every Thursday afternoon with some of the town's elite women. Big Jack was the house butler who had worked for the Riggers plantation for 20 years and as usual, he served mint juleps and finger sandwiches at 2:00 p.m., as the women chatted and fanned in the sweltering summer heat.

Teasing Marian was the highlight of the afternoon as the ladies commented about Big Jack's ebony black skin, magnificent body and keen features. His physique seemed chiseled in the butler's uniformed white shirt, black tie, pants and dress coat. It irritated them when Marian excused Big Jack after he served the refreshments.

Their miniscule minds and busy, gossiping mouths always speculated there was an intimate relationship between Marian and her butler.

But of course, Marian would abruptly dismiss their accusations by coercively changing the conversation with her version of other town gossip.

Born Abioye, meaning born into royalty and given the slave name Cornelius, the nick name "Big Jack" was given by Marian's late husband, after he single-handedly killed a mule that went bonkers after grazing in and ingesting some loco weed. The mule made the mistake of kicking Master Riggers.

Big Jack actually ran the home including the hiring and firing of help, ordering and distribution of supplies, the buying and selling of crops and settled any disputes amongst the workers.

Three days earlier he hired an elderly black woman to help Marian tend her flower and vegetable gardens, she was certain to win first prize again this year for her cabbage because they were as usual, the largest in the region.

As the sun set and a tranquil evening breeze brushed across the porch, Big Jack brought Marian a cold glass of lemonade and they sat on the porch; he in the corner rocking chair and she in the faded swing chatting back and forth about tomorrow's events. Big Jack's quarters were in an old storage room on the ground floor with meager furnishings. It was cold as ice in the winter and hot as fish grease during the summer. As Marian talked about the old woman Big Jack had thought about letting her go because she made a disturbing statement which made him terribly uncomfortable. The old woman told him that *all secrets have ears and the Possum Ridge curse would soon be upon the Rigger's House.* Rather than follow his instincts, Big Jack thought about how Marian loved the way the old woman gardened and had expressed her approval so he allowed her to remain.

Big Jack did not believe in the superstitious stories of witchcraft passed along by generations of slaves though he wore a Juju charm around his neck and hung a horseshoe outside his bedroom above

20

the door frame. The horse shoe and charm was believed of West African slaves to protect against witchcraft and to bring good luck.

As he settled in for the evening his mind drifted to the old woman and how peculiar she was. She reminded him of the old Shamans of his childhood. But that was a time long ago and he soon drifted off to sleep. Marian came to his room in a beautiful sleeping gown and climbed into bed with Big Jack as she'd done since the night her husband died. Big Jack no longer refused her intimacy for they both had fallen into a forbidden love that could never leave the walls of that room. As always, Marian returned to her lavish bedroom with its rugged cypress wood bed frame and posts and the huge revolving oval mirror of which she could see her reflection from head to toe. As always, before she retired for the evening she flipped the mirror so it faced the bedroom wall.

The next morning Big Jack knocked on Marian's bedroom door simultaneously as he used one hand to open the door balancing the tray with the other. He'd prepared coffee, biscuits, gravy, ham and fresh eggs. She was dressing behind the screen putting on her summer dress for the day's festivities. As she appeared from behind the dressing screen, Big Jack dropped the tray and food splattered on the floor and over his shoes. He grabbed her by the arms as the mirror flipped forward and shouted with great anger demanding to know what she was doing in Marian's room. She snatched herself away from his grip and twirled around in front of the mirror and screamed. She did not see her beautiful face but the face of an old black woman. Marian tried to speak but nothing was physically as it should be.

The Sheriff was summoned and Big Jack and the old black woman standing where Marian once stood were cuffed and placed in jail. He was the last to see Marian alive and now she was missing and no one could explain her disappearance.

The Negros working the plantation was extremely jealous and angry of Big Jack's status and preferential treatment. They plotted, hired and arranged for the old Sharman to cast a spell on Marian to put an end to what they saw as an unethical and defiled relationship. The

Sharman used her own hair and hair from Marian's hair brush along with willow bark, argue root, organic powders, bones and other ghastly ingredients conjuring a potion which was served with three drops in Marian's mint julep. The spell and potion was known as "The Transformation" and only chief Sharman could cast such a spell.

The Sheriff tried to question the old woman but she appeared deranged. Since Marian's disappearance the Sharman could no longer talk so she wildly flung about and gestured like she had lost her mind. Big Jack learned first-hand that all secrets have ears and the possum ridge curse was alive and real.

Witchcraft is real and to dabble in it can cost you more than you bargain for. Beware of Palm readers, fortune tellers, card readers, daily horoscope and the occult.

CHAPTER - 4

DIVINE INTERVENTION

The Rodney King riot started in South Los Angeles in 1992 within the Los Angeles Metropolitan area in California. It eventually spread out into other surrounding areas over a six-day period. The riots started on April 29th after a trial jury acquitted four Los Angeles Police Department officers of assault and use of excessive force. The officers were videotaped beating Rodney King an African-American motorist, after a high-speed police pursuit. Thousands of people throughout the metropolitan area in Los Angeles rioted over six days following the announcement of the verdict. Racial tension between the Police Department and the African-American community did not help detour the festering rage.

The Rodney King trial was the office talk of the day and it was also hump day and Melanie was looking forward to getting home. Ten hour days, better known as the 4/40 were still an adjustment and seemed long even though she had every Friday off. There was no dance, sports practices or music classes for the kids so she could actually go straight home, non-stop. Melanie noticed there were a lot of people hanging out on the corners. She dreaded the freeway which would be a faster route and preferred Figueroa Street south, Florence west, maneuvering to Van Ness Boulevard.

As she was tuning her radio there was a strong urge in her spirit to avoid Florence Avenue although it cut off a great deal of traffic. "Where are all these people going," she thought as she continued driving and fumbling with the radio. It was usually tuned to KNX 1070 Radio but one of the kids must have switched stations. "How many times do I have to tell them kids not to mess with my radio," she said aloud. "Dang, now I've passed Florence," she muffled. The radio finally tunes in with a breaking report: "...unrest is developing all over the city because of the "not guilty" verdict in the Rodney King trial.

Officers Koon, Wind, and Briseno were acquitted of all charges.
The jury acquitted the fourth officer, (Powell), on the assault with a deadly weapon charge but failed to reach a verdict on the use of excessive force charge. The jury deadlocked at 8-4 in favor of acquittal. Hoodlums in the intersection of Florence and Normandie Avenue were shooting in the air with rifles and throwing rocks at passing cars…"

The closer Melanie got to home the more people were piling onto the streets shouting and waving their fists into the air. "Thank God there were no classes today and my family should be home safe," she thought. Her mouth is getting dry and palms are sweating on the wheel as she navigates cautiously through the streets towards home. She prays silently for protection of herself, family and City of Los Angeles.

Finally she pulls into her driveway, puts the car in park, turns off the engine, quickly scrambles as she gathers her things and exits the car. Her husband and children were waiting in the doorway relieved she was finally home and safe.

Everyone was talking excitedly at once the children with, "Mom it's a riot!" "We are so scared!" Then her husband says thoughtfully, "Babe, I was so worried, come look at the television people are going crazy out there!"

Melanie drops her purse and belongings on the couch and rushes into the bedroom with her family. She sits at the foot of her bed in front of the television watching the news report. "Oh my God," she Whispers covering her mouth with her hands while tears stream down her face. "Had I taken Florence today, I would've been in the vicinity of that truck driver!" She turns and faces her kids and husband and said, "God told me not to take Florence today!"

They all bunched up on the foot of the bed hugging and watched as the city was overtaken with chaos, looting and rioting.

CHAPTER - 5

CAN'T GET INVOLVED

Alyssa is a black, single parent and often has male visitors that spend the night and leave early the next morning. Margaret, the next door neighbor's kitchen window faces the west side of Alyssa's house and the front and back of the house are also in clear view.

It was always obvious when she was entertaining company because her six-year old daughter Olivia played outside in the yard for extended hours on school nights, and most of the day and evening on weekends.

The latest visitor was a mean-natured man Alyssa called BJ and his only interaction with Olivia was verbally and physically abusive. Whenever Alyssa left her daughter alone with this man he would beat her. Margaret could hear the child's cries clearly after each lick of the swinging belt until the crying ceased, and him shouting, "I told you I would get you!"

Margaret kept to herself, tended to her own business and did not like getting involved in the business of others. The beatings continued and she often turned her music up to drown out the child's cries.

A few weeks passed since the beatings started and a neighbor from across the street paid Margaret a visit, informing her that six-year old Olivia had died. She was walking home alone from school and a huge, black dog began chasing her. Frightened of the dog Olivia ran into the busy street and was struck and killed instantly by a car. The driver did not see her in time and could not stop.

This was horrible news for Margaret because Olivia was so young and innocent. But maybe it was God's way of saving her from those horrible beatings. Margaret thought, "How could I get involved when my husband beats our sons the same way?

CHAPTER - 6

AT THE 25TH HOUR

Kai Harbor and her children lived with her parents in a three-bedroom home. Quentin her son, slept in her brother's room sharing twin beds and she and Christina slept in her old bedroom on a Riviera corner piece sofa bed. Kai was a teen mom sowing her wild oats on weekends at popular clubs. After she put her children to bed she would leave and return before morning. Her mother did not mind, she knew Kai was young and restless but she was a good mother to her children. They usually never woke up once they went to sleep so it never posed a problem.

This Friday night Kai decided to stay in and go to bed early. Christina was sound asleep cuddling her stuffed teddy bear and the crackling snow on the television watched Kai as she began to dream. Of all things she dreams about a party. It was a crowded house party and the overflow of people filtered into the front and back yards. It was odd because Kai did not frequent house parties since she could get into clubs. Loud R & B music from the 70's played on the stereo with the volume blasting. The bass could be felt reverberating off the walls and floor. People were doing the latest dances as musk mixed with sweat and smoke filled the room. They were grooving to the latest hits by Aretha Franklin, Roberta Flack, Wilson Picket, Al Green and the Spinners.

It was not strange for anyone to puke in the bushes and a fight to break out between two losers who had too much to drink. Kai did not recognize any of the people at the party; she could not remember how she got there but needed a way home. She spotted a beige touch tone telephone sitting atop a buffet and decided to call someone to pick her up. She called her parent's house and her dad answered, strangely she looked at the phone as he gave his usual party lecture. It was difficult hearing him above the background noises but she heard him say he would be there around 6:00 a.m. (it was 11:30 p.m.) "Whatever," she thought as she placed the receiver down.

"Ouch," she said as she was abruptly awakened by the 1971 Sylmar 6.5 earthquake, which caused the phone receiver to fall off the overhead corner dividing table and hit her on the forehead. Shocked confused and experiencing pain; rubbing her head she frowned as she looked at the clock radio; it was 5:59 a.m.

"I was dreaming," Kai thought. Dad was coming to get me at ... but wait; he died three years ago," as she abruptly sits straight up in bed.

CHAPTER – 7

A DAY IN THE OFFICE

The Facilities Management Division moved for the third time in twelve months due to budget adjustments, downsizing and departmental merging. Pearl, one of six administrative assistants has been with the department for 21 years. Alhambra was the furthest location she'd had to travel to from her home. Her travel time was never under one-hour and that was in ideal traffic conditions. Though she despised the move she was happy to have employment with all the recent layoffs and to see friends from her earlier years of service at this new location.

Well-liked by everyone Pearl was always the same no matter what was happening in her life or in the office. People were comfortable confiding in her because of her wisdom and confidentiality. As in most office environments there is at least one person everyone labels as strange, weird or just different. The one most voted in Pearl's unit was Susan, a Caucasian woman labeled strange mostly because of her overt promiscuity, especially with men of color.

Susan felt comfortable talking with Pearl because she was never judgmental. During one of these times of sharing she mentioned her two children, a boy and girl and how she'd given them up for adoption because she could not properly care for them. They live in Canada and the adoption is open so she is able to be a part of their lives. Susan visits her children 2-3 times a year and calls and sends them gifts. Pearl knew it was not finances that caused her to give up her children because she made real good money but Susan never said and Pearl never pried.

Pearl often wondered what bible the other office saints read when it came to dealing with Susan. Since religiosity was evident she also wondered why they had the gall to separate themselves completely from her because of lifestyle differences.

29

They always talked negatively and judgmentally when it concerned Susan. If they knew her story they might better understand her character. It should be obvious to her co-workers that she knew nothing about genuine love.

Susan borrowed and read a Christian book Pearl had on her desk that dealt with releasing your past. Although she was not a professed Christian the book helped and blessed her.

It was evident she was a bit psychotic, depressed and tormented but she did her work, kept to herself and her work ethic was spotless; she rarely took off, was never late and would work over time if the need arose.

It was Monday morning and Susan had showered and was dressing for work as usual. She placed a letter for her children in an addressed, stamped envelope and sealed it. She released her bird Charlie from its cage and let the cat out. Went into her garage and climbed into her 82' Toyota Corolla and headed for work, five miles from her apartment. As usual, she parks in an assigned parking space, gathered her things, exits the car and takes the elevator to the 4th floor. In the reception area she placed the letter for her children in the outgoing box for U.S. mail.

The monthly staff meeting was today at 10:00 a.m. in the conference room, always the third Wednesday of the month. Her unit consisted of three managers and 15 staff employees. With the exception of the managers the staff sat in tight cubicles with petitions separating them. Not very private and sometimes frustrating because she generally had to deal with harsh comments made from one side and sometimes loud gospel music from the other. At 9:45 a.m. she took the Glock 9 millimeter semi-automatic pistol from her purse, (which she purchased six-weeks prior) and usually kept under the driver's seat of her car. Susan leaves her office space and on either side opens fire on the employees killing them both. They were often referred to as the wicked witches of the office. She then turned towards the manager's office where the assistant manager was also sitting (like a two-for-one sell) and shot them both. By this time the entire office is now in full panic mode. They could not see over their petitions and were not sure of the direction the gun firing was coming. As some staff began to flee they ran into Susan pleading with a (I'm going to die look in their eyes) and she fired again killing three more.

She heard a rustling sound as she turned and it was Pearl. Each time the weapon fired the sound seemed closer to Pearl's desk. In the chaos and in a panic Pearl thought she would try and run but not soon enough. Susan had this blank stare in her eyes as she thanked her for always being nice to her, and pointed the gun and fired…

The letter to her children read:

> Dear Chloe and Reggie:
>
> By the time you receive this I will be gone. I have struggled with rationality most of my life and could not do it anymore. No one has ever really liked me and the only love I've known is the love I have for the two of you.
>
> I hope you will forgive me for what I have done but it was my only way out.
>
> Love
> Susan

As the police set up a perimeter for the CSI (crime scene investigators), the coroner brought out the last of the eight victims as the detectives were taking Pearl's statement.

Pearl turned her head slightly and squeezed her eyes tightly as Susan pressed down on the trigger but the gun clicked and misfired. Her life seemed to flash before her like a movie in slow motion.

31

Susan immediately turned the gun on herself, as she pulled the trigger and it fired.

CHAPTER - 8

AN APPARITION

It is said that the process of grieving over the loss of a loved one gets better with time and that is usually true, but Yolanda finds herself from time to time still experiencing moments of grief since the loss of her husband. Almost two years have passed and she is progressing as she continues to love him, remembers their lives together and learns to live without him.

Hectically looking for a computer file that he would instinctively know how to find Yolanda thought about how much she missed them working on projects together. Their home-based business allowed them to be creative together and to help others who were just starting up small businesses or churches by providing competitive, professional graphic services for book marks, logos, business cards, brochures, programs and printed envelopes.

Working on an order of raffle tickets she needed to find this file so she could change the date and would not have to redesign them. Sitting down in front of the computer she thought aloud, *"Babe, you know where this file is and I could really use your help."*

Almost immediately she felt a strong overwhelming presence in the room as she slowly exhaled. Peering over her left shoulder at the fold-up chair he used when he sat with her appeared a shear silhouette that resembled her late husband, dressed in an almost indescribable material appearing to be a soft white, silky shirt and pants. He was a healthy weight, muscular with male patterned baldness and he looked well. His essence seemed to fill the room and this experience was all of five seconds but seemed as though at that moment time had stood still.

Yolanda remembered a preacher saying once in a message that we could not reach the dead after they've gone and they do not try to contact us. Any such event would be a trick of the enemy.

She couldn't remember the scriptural text he used to support his statement and honestly at that moment did not care.

The apparition was as real to her as life itself. When she turned back to the computer she immediately went to the file she had been searching for all morning. Though grieving, she was of sound mind and did not believe in ghost or sorcery but wholeheartedly believed in God, His Word, heaven and hell the whole nine yards.

There was no attempt at verbal exchange or extra sensory perception (thank God) because she would have still been running down the streets. She sensed he was alright where he was and she needed to continue living her life.

The experience left her pondering over how it did not matter what her peers, theologians, or anyone else might think when she shared this experience. She knew without a doubt, her consciousness was cognizant and was fully aware as she was consumed in awe of the encounter she just had.

CHAPTER - 9

HEARING FROM GOD

Walking on the sand at the water's edge is peaceful and liberating, especially during the early morning hours. The risen sun and its rays sparkle as they hop across recessing waves. The ocean air is cool, clear, crisp and fresh whether jogging, running, or walking and you meet all sorts of people coming and going.

Rachael walked the beach three to four days a week for 30-40 minutes: 15-20 minutes each way. Halfway through she always hoped the flock of birds in front of the lifeguard's station would disperse before she got too close to them. There would be so many seagulls and a small flock of a strange looking grey bird with long thin legs that reminded Rachael of stilts. All sorts of species were scuffling after the pieces of bread the elderly couple left daily. The coastline also seemed to inspire the invasion of people walking their pets, bike riders, skateboarders and those on inline skates.

Ocean Boulevard is home to tall office buildings, condominiums and apartments, restaurants, a Convention and Entertainment Center, Aquarium of the Pacific, Shoreline Drive all making it a tourist and residents paradise.

The scenic view is breathtaking and there are few, if any, distractions. For Rachael, this day was much like times before with the exception of a woman sitting in the sand dressed in what seemed to be office attire; rust colored linen pants, a soft white blouse, and bare feet with black pumps lying beside her in the sand. As Rachael passed she spoke softly and the woman seemed preoccupied as she nodded back. There was a quickening in Rachael as she passed. A strong *spirit of suicide was felt* as she continued walking. The spirit was pulling and tugging on her so strongly she could no longer concentrate or return to worshipping and talking with God. The woman's knees were tucked under her chin as her arms wrapped around the front of her legs clutching her hands.

The blank like stare pierced straight ahead as if hypnotized by the ocean's waves.

Rachael was reaching the halfway point and about to turn around for the last twenty minutes of her walk when God told her to tell the woman sitting in the sand, "Your situation is not hopeless, remember God loves you." Rachael began silently challenging God with excuses: "I don't know her; she is going to think I am bonkers." Again, God instructed Rachael to tell her exactly what He was telling her to say. She was approaching the spot the woman was occupying and the spirit of suicide was even heavier than before. She quickly walked over to the woman and proceeded to tell her what God had said. "Uh excuse me, God told me to tell you that your situation is not hopeless and remember God loves you." Immediately Rachael sensed in the spirit realm weights seem to float off the woman's shoulders. She looked up with tears streaming down her face and said, "Thank you, thank you so much!" She picked up her shoes, stood up and dusted the sand from her pants and ran quickly towards the parking lot. She stopped, sat on the cement wall and dusted her feet as she put on her black pumps. Then she stood up, crossed the parking lot and disappeared into the office building.

What Rachel did not know was that this woman prayed for the first time in her life, asking God for a miracle and a sign so she would undoubtedly know he heard her prayer.

If you are reading this and you are a Believer, God wants you to be encouraged to hang on and don't give up; if you're not God yet loves you and wants you to be encouraged and never give up.

CHAPTER - 10

THE ENCOUNTER

Reggie truly believes most people who are visibly struggling with life (unemployment, overwhelming debt, homelessness, poverty and hunger) are not always totally responsible for the cave experience they sometimes find themselves in. Downsizing, layoffs, congress and their political games, the unstable economy and more can play a huge role. Over the years he has become more sensitive to those in need. What I mean is, rather than trying to figure out how they got to where they are – his thoughts are what can he do to help or change the situation? It has been said sometimes we all have been or may be just one paycheck away from being homeless.

As a child there were lean times in his home but he never knew they were poor. Never went to bed hungry even though the meal sometimes was a bit lean. The services of the utility companies such as lights, gas and water were sometimes interrupted but his parents made a game of it. They boiled water for bathing, used candles and said they were camping indoors; you name it they said it as to not worry their children. When he was old enough to attend school he saw the difference between poor and lean. Children with holes in their shoes, or no laces, and children lacking the proper clothing for any of the seasons weather conditions. For many children, their only meal was the school breakfast and lunch programs Monday through Friday but balanced meals on weekends and holidays were a mystery.

The homeless population seemed to be growing because he often saw people living literally on the streets, barefoot, filthy and clothes were like rags. Of course, some were drug addicts, alcoholics and others were suffering from mental illness and some were war veterans with PTSD (Post Traumatic Stress Syndrome). These indigent conditions were not only indicative to adults, but families with children were sleeping in their cars or going from motel to motel, because their home mortgage became unmanageable due to the rising housing market and interest rates.

37

Hardly a day goes by that he does not encounter someone begging or asking for help. It has been proven some people make a fairly good living by appealing to the sympathy of others and not everyone who begs is in need. Usually we do not have time or we have too much going on in our own lives to try to help fix the problem so we give aid through a handout and food drives and keep going. Honestly, oftentimes what we witness in the plight of others is just too devastating to deal with. It's like turning the television channel when they air commercials with children dying from starvation, disease and contaminated water in third world countries. The empathy is there but we do not want to see the grave conditions.

One must be cautious because not everyone that asks for help is in need. Once at a carwash a man had a broken key. He stated all he needed was seventy-five cents and he would be able to get a new key made for his car. He genuinely appeared as though he was having a moment of misfortune. Reggie gave him two-dollars only to see this same man in front of Vons the next week with the same key.

Yet there was another occasion of which his wife Shelby shared which happened at the lunch truck on her job. There is a lot of derelicts downtown, but the people that worked in her building often bought the homeless food. One of her co-workers brought a homeless man a sandwich and he threw it on the ground and cursed the man because he wanted the money. People will often offer to pay for food rather than give money to prevent the person in need from using the money to buy drugs or alcohol.

Reggie was a generous man and people with their hand out usually received a response from him. As people sometimes say, "They saw him coming." His wife Shelby on the other-hand was not so easy. Actually, she almost never gave. She had a way of being politely rude as she swiftly walked passed someone begging. She's had two life-changing encounters that she and Reggie believe were orchestrated by God because of her gross lack of empathy.

Shelby was working full-time and continuing her college education at night. She attended school one night a week and all day two

Saturdays per month. One Saturday on her way to class she stopped for breakfast with five dollars to last her the day. She had broken a twenty dollar bill and given five dollars each to the children and five dollars to her husband Reggie.

Shelby stopped at McDonald's to purchase an Egg McMuffin and small coffee which would cost a little over two-dollars. As she pulled into the parking stall she saw a young Caucasian girl about the same age as her own daughter standing outside the doors. It was cold; she was shaking and seemed scared. Her clothing was soiled, she wore a white tattered t-shirt that had tiny blood stains on it; hair was matted and she wore khaki pants and bare feet. This is Shelby's account of the encounter:

As I passed the girl and proceeded to enter the restaurant, an overwhelming compassion overcame me. I continued inside but could not stop thinking about the young girl outside. "What happened to her? Where was her mother and was she worried? Was anyone looking for her?" I could not imagine my own daughter being stranded, needing help or being in this predicament. My stomach began churning and my eyes were beginning to tear. There were three people ahead of me in line and when the cashier asked me if she could take my order I said without thinking, "One Egg McMuffin breakfast meal with orange juice and a small coffee please." After paying for the order and collecting my change I proceeded out the door towards my car but I stopped and gave the young girl the meal. She had tears in her eyes and said, "Thank You." For a long time I was angry with myself for not trying to help further but I did not know what to do. I'd never allowed myself to have compassion for anyone or to give them a handout. Of course, now I am bawling as I entered the freeway onramp. I prayed for her. I earnestly, fervently prayed for her.

Classes on Saturday were ten hours so not only did I not have breakfast but no money for lunch. Figured I could survive off nuts, sunflower seeds and water. Right before lunch one of my classmates asked me if she could take me to lunch and discuss the upcoming group project. I never knew what happened to that child and it plagued me for a while. I believe that because it was ignorance on my part and yet I was obedient to the Spirit of God on her behalf the prayers of the righteous availed much and she was rescued.

Second encounter was sometime later as I was entering a Ralph's grocery store. It was on a Friday evening after work and I was tired but we needed to stock up. There was a woman outside the store with two teen girls. She was hesitant to approach me and did not approach everyone entering the store. The girls stood back as the mother cautiously moved towards me. She said, "Excuse me mam, but my daughters and I just left an abusive relationship and we are trying to get enough gas to reach San Diego." Pointing behind her she said, "Those are my daughters and we left everything we own behind." I took the time to tell her I did not have any cash but when I was done with my shopping I would give her something (I'd never stopped long enough to listen to anyone's plight) usually I just rushed past. The emotional knob in my mind would usually be set between the mode of prejudging and not wanting to be bothered.

They did not look or appear homeless. They looked as normal as anyone else entering the market to purchase food. They were not dirty nor were their clothes tattered. The lady was very apprehensive as someone who had not had experience in having to ask a stranger for help.

As I entered the turnstile that overwhelming feeling of compassion hit me. Stopping abruptly and taking out my wallet I gave my husband a five dollar bill to go back and give to the woman. He rushed out the store as if I might have a change of heart and would want to retrieve the five-dollars. When he returned he said with sarcasm, "I know this is God because you do not give to anyone and now you are giving five-dollars!" As we continued shopping my mind drifted back to the woman and her daughters. Genuine concern and compassion rose up in my spirit. As we left the market, I took another twenty dollars out and gave it to the woman and she said with tearful eyes, "Thank you mam, may God bless you for your generosity." Needless to say my husband thought I'd had a nervous breakdown or something.

There have been other encounters but these two were life changing and I learned valuable lessons on both occasions. God wants us to be cautious and wise but He also does not want us to lack compassion for others. God used me not just to help someone in need, but to help me as He changed my heart and mindset towards those in need. Changing my heart to be compassionate and to be willing to act in obedience to God was necessary for me to do the kind of Kingdom work God had destined me for.

I always ask God for clarity and discernment and I remember the scripture:

Hebrew 13:2 (NIV) Don't forget to show hospitality to strangers, for some who have done this have entertained angels without realizing it!

In the bible hospitality was an important virtue for Christians and leaders. But because of this free offer of hospitality Christians had to be aware of perpetrators trying to take advantage of their generosity. It is the same today and discernment is important. This life changing experiences motivated Shelby to organize a semi-annual can drive on campus and donated the items to a food kitchen for the homeless. Her heart was pruned and primed and she was open to and continues working on ideas and volunteering to help others in the community. There is an impartation and overflow of that spirit today (some thirty years later) in Shelby's daughter and granddaughter. They can always be found giving money, food, and clothing, whatever they have to others that are in need.

CHAPTER – 11

BREAKDOWN

They were childhood sweethearts; Doris was employed by the Board of Education and Calvin an officer with the Sheriff Department. This was quite the achievement for the late 60's especially for people of color. Though Doris was reared in a very stringent Christian environment neither she nor Calvin attended church. For Doris, there were just too many restrictions. She always liked to party and have an occasional drink which was strictly forbidden as a member of the church or in her parent's home.

For a young couple they were prosperous and lived in an apartment building her father owned on the east side of town. Unfortunately, her recurring infidelity lead to her divorce from Calvin and then moving in with and later marrying Ricco, the one she cheated on Calvin with. Though Calvin was hurt he eventually moved on.

Doris suffered five miscarriages with Ricco, each pregnancy surviving one month longer than the previous. There is a cliché that says, "What goes around comes around," and it seemed that way for Doris. Her second marriage to Ricco ended after a few short years, he left Doris for another woman. One would think this would be enough to cause her mind to snap but her mental deterioration begins long before her troubled marriages. But as it was in those times, it was unheard of or unacceptable to seek psychiatric help, even when family suspected you had a problem it was simply ignored.

The signs were there when Doris could not keep a job. She went from a prestigious position with the Board of Education (right before she was to receive a promotion), to working for ABC Markets (working in the booth), to a continued pattern of unemployment. While working for the neighborhood market, family would frequent the store and sometimes Doris acted as though they were strangers. Out of guilt she would call a few days later crying and apologizing, not understanding why she'd ignored them.

Possibly trying to get a grip on reality she rededicated her life to God and attended the family church which was a Missionary Baptist Church, a very traditional Baptist Church. But her way of praise and adoration was different than the members were use too. Had she been in an Apostolic or Church of God in Christ she would have fit right in but her way of praise lasted too long during service and was viewed more as a disruption. Sadly, a group of busy-bodied, self-righteous saints had a meeting with the pastor and deacons and voted to relinquish Doris' membership. Unimaginable! Church is the place where people go to receive from God, to find solace and peace while seeking hope. Yet, a small group of members held a secret meeting and voted to revoke her membership and it was then she really began to mentally decline.

Doris stayed with various family members for a season but her unstable mental condition continued deteriorating and erratic behavior increased. We have come a long way with our outlook and education concerning mental illness but during Doris' time those closes to her had no idea what the signs were for depression or Schizophrenia. There were a myriad of clinically diagnosable things happening in the mind of Doris but ignorance and pride had everyone look the other way or pretend nothing was wrong.

She was in and out of hospitals and facilities for the mentally ill but she was so cunning she could talk the skin off an onion. She'd take the medication, say what they wanted to hear and the facilitators and doctors thought she was improving and she would be discharged.

Doris drove a powdered blue Volkswagen beetle and she would take these sporadic drives oftentimes ending in her detainment in hospitals in other cities. Her siblings would go to her rescue, sign her out and she would seem alright for a while and off she'd go again. Refusing or neglecting to take her prescribed medications contributed to the reoccurrences of erratic behavior.

It always seems as though God had Angels watching over her because she was never robbed or assaulted.

A couple of truck drivers found her in her beetle on the side of a road leading to Las Vegas and called the local Sheriff. The officers and truck drivers spoke to family of how dangerous it was for her to travel the way she did. The family knew this but they could not control or contain her. After a few episodes of Doris' *trips* she lost the car and was forced to settle in town. The family would find her placement in special care facilities or transitional housing and when she got tired, she left.

Finally, she becomes homeless and a "bag lady" pushing a shopping cart up and down the streets. The family usually knew her hang outs and they would check on her often to make sure she was safe as they soon gave up on trying keeping her off the streets. The talk in half whispers and hushed tones was she'd had a nervous breakdown. Actually they did not know what a nervous breakdown was. That is not even a clinical term in the world of mental illness but I suppose it is better than saying she's crazy as hell. It's a metaphoric term. Cars and machines break down, but in her case so do people. It was as though something broke or misfired in the mind of Doris.

Her behavior became more erratic and unpredictable. Although it was visually obvious she had a problem she was cunning. The State gave her a disability check and she was sane enough to handle her own banking. She had a checking and savings account and if the lines were long when she went into the bank, she would rant and rave, cursing and terrifying the customers thus reducing the length of the lines because customers felt threatened and left. By the time police officers arrived she was calm, as if nothing happened as she continued to handle her banking business.

Doris was so well known most of the proprietors in the neighborhood had her sister Peggy's phone number and would call her first whenever a problem developed before they would call the police. On holidays Peggy would pick Doris up so she could clean up, change clothes and have dinner with the family. Overtime, Doris refused to have anything to do with the family but she would show up in Peggy's neighborhood (usually at odd hours of the morning and night) causing a huge disturbance waking up the entire neighborhood with her rampant shouting and frantic delirium. Peggy's children were afraid of their aunt Doris because of her erratic behavior and the fact she would threaten them. Consequently Doris was no longer welcomed in the neighborhood or Peggy's home.

There were many years she spent living on the streets with her shopping cart she called her "Cadillac." It was filled with plastic bags, bottles of rubbing alcohol, old tattered clothing, imperishable food items, filthy blankets and other stuff. At times, she would moon passing cars on main highways, or she would drop her pants and defecate anywhere she felt; oftentimes she would talk to imaginary people but she always knew and recognized her family. When it was beneficial for her or when she did not want to be bothered she would deliberately cause a ruckus.

Before the battle began in her mind she was a physically beautiful, stately woman with a deep chocolate skin tone. But life on the streets has a way of causing premature aging and progressive deterioration. Extreme temperatures, poor hygiene, unhealthy diet, the absence of the essentials of life all play a part.

One cold winter morning her sister Peggy received the final call, Doris had passed away in the night while sleeping on a bus bench. It was freezing temperatures and that night it got below 30 degrees.

Ironically Doris was not the only family member whose elevator did not go all the way up but the others got by somehow. It was a generational curse because most of Peggy's female siblings were strange in their own way with similar systemically mentally declining characteristics.

This is beyond learned behavior; many children learn to be messy if their parents are messy. But generational curses are a spiritual bondage that is passed down from one generation to another. Symptoms of a generational curse can include a continual negative pattern of something being handed down from generation to generation like in Doris' case mental illness.

46

Generational curses are so real people who are adopted end up with the same characteristics as their birth parents, not because they were around their birth parents to learn how they behaved, but because they inherited their spiritual bondage. For reference purposes read Genesis 34:7 and Lamentations 5:7.

Some common symptoms of generational curses are family illnesses that seem to just pass from one person down to the next (cancer is a common physical manifestation of a spiritual bondage), continued infidelity, continued financial difficulties, mental illnesses such as persistent irrational fears and depression. My Lord! Anything that seems to be a persistent struggle or problem that was handed down from one generation to another may very well be a generational curse.

Statistically, one of four adults over eighteen suffer from some sort of mental disorder that is diagnosable and treatable. It is the leading cause of disabilities in the United States and Canada. Is that not alarming?

As mentioned earlier the majority of Doris' family were practicing Christians (well some were just religious). Nonetheless, one of the younger relatives recognized the pattern in the family's history and did some research sharing her findings with the other cousins. Whether they all took heed by praying to break the generational curse from having a stronghold in their children is not known. But I suppose all one needs to do is assess the remaining females. Next time you are at a family reunion, picnic, wedding or dinner, check out the history and check out the now...how many 51-50's do you see? Size 'em up. Remember, one of four adults over eighteen suffer from some sort of mental disorder. Look around you; one, two, three and... four...

CHAPTER – 12

CROWS IN THE BACKYARD

Mr. Moore is a very superstitious man probably because his parents and subsequent generations were superstitious about everything. They wore dimes in their shoes to keep people from casting spells on them and the women would not place their handbags on the floor because the superstition is that you will always be broke. He remembers one of his dads friends would not go into his own house because he believed his wife sprinkled some sort of voodoo powder around the house. Mr. Moore's dad had to go inside to retrieve the friend's clothes. There were many other superstitions in his family especially concerning death:

❖ If a robin flies in the house through an open window, death will soon follow.

❖ You must hold your breath when passing a cemetery or you might breathe in the spirit of one who has recently died.

❖ If a clock which has not been working suddenly chimes, there will be a death in the family.

❖ If a dead person's eyes are left open, he would find someone to take with him.

One of the most prolific superstitions is the crow being a bringer of death. Not only is this a superstition but whether in a movie, or novel crows always represented something evil. Crows and ravens are unattractive, stout black birds with long bills and legs. Even the vocal sound they make is eerie. With all of their physical misfortune they have been found to be highly intelligent, especially in a group.

Whenever Mr. Moore's aunt Millie saw crows in her backyard the superstitious belief was within three days someone they knew well would die and it never failed. Though it was not every day she saw

49

crows in her yard she believed their visit brought death. The legend is to see a single crow is unlucky, two crows signified good luck, three crows meant health, four crows wealth, five sickness and six or more meant death. All Moore remembers is the six or more. Most superstitions to those who do not believe are recognized more as fallacies, delusions or misconceptions but to Moore it was the real deal. The death was not necessarily going to be within their family but someone they knew well would die.

His first experience was at the age of eight standing in the kitchen with his aunt Millie. As she looked out the window into the backyard she grabs her shirt collar with both hands saying, "Oh my Lord, them crows are gathering, somebody gone surely die." Three days later his uncle Roger bites the dust; dies in his sleep. It happened again when he was in his early twenties. While watching television his mom was on the back porch when she saw a group of crows. Three days later, a neighbor passed away.

Throughout his life crows have always been associated with death, especially in the gathering of six or more. Now Moore is fifty and he pulls into his own driveway and sees a flock of crows gathered in his backyard under an old oak tree. It's been a while and it was usually in the home of someone else that the crow gathering occurred. He thought aloud, "The crows again, someone must be going to die." Moore picked up a stick from the yard and threw it in the direction of the crows so they would fly away. They scattered quickly as they squawked making the most unsettling sound for a bird.

Once inside his house Moore called his cousins and told them about the crows he saw in his yard. They laughed and teased him saying he would now carry the banner as the bearer of the crows in the family. The following morning Moore's phone rang repeatedly while his car was still parked in the drive way. The cousin he last spoke with found him dead three days later sitting in his favorite chair reading the paper.

CHAPTER - 13

GIRL WITH A BABY

During the late 60's the statistics for teen mothers between ages 15–19 were 70.3 per every 1,000 births. The greatest decline occurred in 2010 from seven decades of 9%, but the United States still rates amongst the highest in teen pregnancy of all the industrialized countries. Society, the home nor the church were addressing it from a practical stance or presenting healthy preventive measures (aside from abstinence). Most Christian parents ignored the subject or used biblical damnation, myths and scare tactics to coerce celibacy in young girls.

Lee Ann represents a typical middle class, Christian family during this period. The family roots dating back to her great-grandparents are two-thirds Cherokee Indian, and a one-third combination of white and black. Her husband, Ryon Sr. was unemployed due to illness and she joined the work force, working the night shift to make ends meet. Prior to this she was a full-time mother and homemaker. Their three children were self-sufficient and the two eldest sons Sémaj and Ryon, Jr. had part-time jobs after school. Each of her children's names was partially influenced by their Cherokee ancestry. Aleihs, the only girl was the youngest. She was smart, independent and somewhat rambunctious but never gave her parents much trouble. Her brothers were jealous of her because their father was always boasting about how well she did in school. This created sibling rivalry and the brothers teased and tormented Aleihs every chance they got. They enjoyed annoying her even though it would result in parental repercussion and punishment.

At the age of 16 Aleihs was allowed to have male company as long as a parent was home. This was decades before cellular phones, call waiting, laptops and multiple land lines in the home. It was understood by everyone in the house, phone usage was limited because there was only one landline.

Conversations were usually brief and calls for minor children were screened and had to occur between certain hours.

As we've progressed from the 60's we find puberty in girls can begin as early as age nine (pubic hair and breast development). The body is preparing itself for the next phase which is menses. Physical changes began taking place due to hormonal stimulation. Menses begins usually a year or so after pubic hair develops. It is at this time girls can conceive. With early development comes the propensity for sexual arousal, experimenting or plain old inquisitiveness. This would be a good time for mother's to monitor their daughter's development, talked with them about changes that occur during their development and share written material. The old way of using religious threats, following her monthly cycle on a calendar, old wives tales or making a young girl feel abnormal because of rising sexual interest is unhealthy.

Lee Ann and Ryon Sr. were trying to give some sort of balance to Aleihs physical and psychological development and her interest in boys. They both agreed and succumbed to supervised visits. These were restricted to a Saturday or Sunday afternoon (if there were no evening church services); there were always Sunday evening church services. The visits always took place in the living room where there was only one television in the entire house and someone was always watching television in that room. School days were never acceptable unless they were studying together and its time and location was restricted; two-hour maximum at the dining room table. Aleihs always thought the numerous restrictions kept the boys she invited from returning but her brothers would harass and threaten them when they left the house and they would be afraid to return. She finally realized this when she witnessed Ryon Jr., throw one of her friends over the front porch banister on to the lawn. For a while, she gave up on having male company.

Later she met someone in church who was 18. Her parents were not excited because of his age but they allowed it because their families knew one another. Aleihs enjoyed going to church but now she wanted to be there every time the doors opened because this meant

52

she and George could see each other. They attended a very large Methodist church which had a lot of classrooms and meeting rooms in the church and in the educational building adjacent to the church. Neither family allowed their children to hang around outside during church services but some services; especially anniversary services were very lengthy and crowded.

It has been said where there is a will there is a way. Both parents seemed to drop their guard and gave leniency to George and Aleihs because both families were involved in the same church. Some Sundays George would go home after service with Aleihs' family and return for the afternoon service. This arrangement prevented and put a halt to her brothers harassing George as they did the other suitors.

George was 18; smooth, polite and he knew how to impress Aleihs' parents. One Sunday afternoon her mom did not go to the service and Ryon Sr. was not as cautious as Lee Ann. George and Aleihs snuck to one of the many classrooms, locked the door and one thing led to another and her virginity was lost on church property. How ironic is that? Although George used protection it malfunctioned and for four months Aleihs hid her pregnancy with over-sized clothing and by secluding herself in her room. Her mother slept during the day because she worked nights and Ryon Sr. was ailing with diabetes and cancer. She did all she could not to draw any extra attention to herself. She even enrolled in summer school but ditched most of the days going to George's house while his parents were at work. Summer sessions did not keep strict attendance records as was done in the fall.

During the first trimester morning sickness was horrendous. She waited for George in front of the hamburger stand next to the school puking her brains out every morning. It was very embarrassing with other students gazing at her as she heaved. On two separate occasions, she tried using and ingesting various popular medicinal remedies rumored to cause miscarriage amongst her peers. They were believed to jump start a girl's menses such as Humphrey's 11 and drinking one-half pint of vodka straight. Because she was vomiting bowl and badly dehydrated the latter landed her a trip to Children's

Hospital where the pregnancy was discovered and reported to her parents by the physician on duty.

As her parents were trying to make sense of this news; after a few intense conversations of which her father argued it was too late to be angry and upset. He thought now more than ever Aleihs needed their emotional support. After a lengthy discussion with George's parents they agreed that George and Aleihs would be married. It was as though marriage would correct or make right the sex and conception before marriage. In God's eyes the baby was conceived out of wedlock, but shot-gun weddings were a common practice during those times. A sixteen year old girl marrying an eighteen year old unemployed young man (neither of the two has finished high school) is not a practical thing to do. What you have is two immature, inexperienced, uneducated and unskilled people keeping house. This is a recipe for disaster.

Some critical thinker once said, "God takes care of babies and fools." Unlike Aleihs' parents, many girls who conceived at her age, were often put out the home or sent away until the baby was born. She was fortunate to have loving and supportive parents. They had spent time imparting and giving Aleihs many nuggets of wisdom that they hoped would help her make the right choice if sex ever presented itself. But she would soon find these nuggets of wisdom necessary to instinctively rely on for her survival and protection.

The young couple moved into George's parent's home and it was indeed a cultural shock. The room was small and stuffy and aside having endless sex it was not very accommodating. Her mother-in-law was not a good cook or housekeeper nor was the food plentiful or healthy. But George soon got a job and they moved into a furnished one-bedroom apartment on the eastside. There she battled with giant water bugs, loneliness and sometimes hunger. George had no idea how to care for a family or any inherent instincts that they should come first, or that he was responsible for their survival and protection.

He borrowed a great deal from his parents and smoked and drank most of his wages. Aleihs was determined to make this work, even with statistical odds that it wouldn't. Consequently, she hid a lot of her suffering (so she thought) from her parents. The couple did not have a telephone and lived quite a distance from either family. When she went into labor, George had to run to the nearest phone booth, call her parents and wait for them to arrive and then transport her to the hospital which was across town. Good thing it was her first child and labor and the birthing process took a while, about seven hours.

Aleihs realized, aside from sex there were many things she did not know about George and they really did not have much in common. He drank, smoked weed, partied, hung with his friends and tried to influence her to do the same, even while pregnant. But her instincts kicked in and she would decline making her more of an outcast.

After physical abuse, negligence and his constant drug usage, she returned to live with her parents. Though Aleihs was very young, she recalled her parental conversations regarding conditions and treatment she should avoid and deem unacceptable. This included things that would put her and her baby at risk such as experimenting with drugs and alcohol, physical or mental abuse, and George's constant unemployment (unwilling to work). George lost jobs because he was always high which caused him to be almost catatonic in the mornings and difficult to wake up for work. Consequently, he was fired because he was excessively late and missed a lot of work days.

Before she moved back home her parents paid her a weekly visit and of course were aware of the conditions she lived in. They prayed and wanted Aleihs to make up her own mind and not be coerced into returning home. During this time they brought groceries, formula and baby food so their daughter and grandchild would not be hungry. George's parents also brought groceries because they too knew their son was not being the provider he should. George's father unfortunately gave him unsound advice. If George was going to go out, he should always come home first, not because he had a family or that he should reframe from adultery and his selfish, raucous lifestyle.

There were times he would be gone over night and there was no phone so Aleihs did not know if he was alright, and he did not seem to care about the welfare of her or the baby. It was the grace of God and the prayers of her family that neither she nor the baby ever became ill during the night.

One evening her brothers overheard their parent's conversation discussing George's unscrupulous treatment of their sister. No one is certain of how they responded but George did keep his distance because he feared her brothers would retaliate.

Though she disappointed her parents and changed the course of her own life she learned a valuable lesson. Because of positive parenting and Christian teaching she had the tools within her to survive and recover. Aleihs was blessed because many young girls that began adulthood at 16 in impoverished conditions become life-long victims of physical and mental abuse, drug and alcohol abuse and experience dangerously low birth weights or still born children.

Although she endured unhealthy conditions for her and her unborn child such as people smoking heavily around her, unknowingly experiencing being contact high her story ends well. Her survival and success is certainly not typical of girls her age. Many die or become trapped in an environment of never ending domestic violence, drug and alcohol abuse, uneducated and impoverished conditions.

We have evolved…or have we? Young girls are still having children out of wedlock but there is no real shame or remorse. It is a common practice and viewed acceptable, even with Christian families as the new norm. Welfare is the system that keeps them in poverty and they no longer marry but live with the fathers of their babies which are usually numerous, resulting in our young men becoming ever more irresponsible, unreliable and disrespectful to women. Some disregard the father all together; they somehow fall out of love after the birth of the baby.

What is the moral of this story? It is still best that we follow the biblical way of procreating and remain celibate until marriage.

Education and preparation, compatibility in all areas of life and beliefs are essential if we are going to be successful at maintaining the traditional American nuclear family, two biological parents and their offspring, which is ordained of God. Pregnancy should never be used as a reason for a couple to marry.

CHAPTER - 14

THE JAZZ MUSICIAN

Jazz is such a uniquely expressed style of music and stands the test of time. It is a music that originated at the beginning of the 20th century within the African-American communities of the Southern United States. Its roots lie in the African-American adoption of European harmony and form to existing African musical elements. Henry Bridges played the saxophone and was a very accomplished jazz musician but at the time we met he no longer played with jazz bands. Unfortunately, in the early church his style of playing and just being affiliated with jazz music was not well accepted. I always enjoyed his instrumental solos because the musical style was different from the normal sounds of church music. As children, my siblings and I were introduced by our mother to various music genres and for that I am grateful. Because of this early exposure we developed an ear and appreciation for the universal sounds of music.

Henry Bridges played with many legendary tenor saxophonists of the late '30s and early '40s such as revolutionary jazz guitarist Charlie Christian and he was considered an excellent saxophone and clarinet player. Bridges might have become a bigger name in the music business had he not been drafted into World War II.

It was said Bridges gigged with both Leslie Sheffield's band and Harlan Leonard in 1939, the latter leader building Bridges a solo at regular intervals in the arrangements. It was service bands in both the United States and Europe that benefited from Bridges' talents until the war ended and he decided to settle in California. He did apparently play a few stages in the '50s, still in fine form, but for the most part left the music scene.

From time to time he tried to add a little cultural music in church services but he was before his time or in the wrong place to be appreciated for his talent.

Church folk have an unsightly way of reacting to and prejudging what they do not like and will not let a person down easy. Mr. Bridges was a well-educated accomplished musician, never haughty and very interesting to talk to and would have been a real asset to the churches music department but some things never change. Rather than recognizing and appreciating his worth and using the gift, the powers that be were threatened and intimidated.

Christians sometimes have the audacity to take unmerited liberties against the spirituality of others. Many a person has been discouraged, wounded and chased away due to graceless tongues. Though we cannot blame others for our falling away hopefully souls won will outweigh the souls that give up. Sadly, many will never know what a musical genius Henry Bridges was. Inflated egos and gross ignorance usually forced closed any potentially open doors within the church.

Ironically, and for many years until his death he developed a curriculum and taught an evangelistic class that met on Wednesday evenings at 6:30 p.m., teaching saints how to witness to others.

At some point (not exactly sure when) his health began to fail him. One Saturday night (or early Sunday morning) I had an unusual dream about Mr. Bridges. In the dream, I was walking down my aunt's neighborhood and there appeared two Angels escorting a golden chariot with six of the most beautiful white horses I'd ever seen, all appearing ten times larger than life. The host and chariot's circumference were so brightly illuminated it was blinding. Peering upward, its size and brightness reminded me of the light of the sun beaming down through giant Sequoia trees when you're on the ground, besides a giant trunk looking up trying to see the tree top. Mr. Bridges was in the chariot and I recognized him by his spirit not by physical features. Dressed in the most beautiful white garment the chariot hovered above me, suspended as he gave me a message for my brother. The message was though he'd been ill he was alright now, and he wanted my brother to continue teaching the evangelism class. The chariot then ascended at warp speed into the heavens. Awakened by my own crying because the dream was so surreal I immediately looked over at the clock it was 4:30 a.m., Sunday morning.

My husband (at the time) heard me crying and I told him about the dream. It was so disturbing I was sobbing almost uncontrollably. Watching the clock realizing it was much too early to call my brother I waited until 6:00 a.m. My brother knew I did not consider myself what some would call or refer to sometimes as a "dreamer," it was rare occasions I had such reveries. However, whenever I experienced dreams so vivid there was usually some validity to them. Bridges had been really ill that past week and we both felt the dream was in reference to his demise. We talked for a few minutes and discontinued our conversation because he needed to make some phone calls and would get back to me later in the day.

Our church choir had to sing at another service at 3:00 p.m. that afternoon. My family and I left after morning service, got a bite to eat and headed for the church we were to fellowship with. When we arrived my husband's (girlfriend...literally but I did not know it at the time) hurried over to me to give the news Mr. Bridges had passed away at 4:30 a.m. this morning. The only people that I shared the dream with were my brother and the man I was then married too. Needless to say, I actually fainted. The news was to devastating and spiritually overwhelming. That was not the best or the most intelligent way to break that kind of news to a person.

His death had me realize there will be people that cross our paths in life we will always remember, and from a music perspective I will always remember and admire the jazz saxophonist Mr. Henry Bridges.

CHAPTER - 15

HEAVEN...

Driving down the 405 freeway as he did five days a week the traffic was moving almost speed limit. Dave was looking forward to the family camping trip to Kings Canyon in Sequoia National Park for a four-day weekend. The giant sequoia trees, fresh mountain air, waterfalls, scenic routes and the beauty of God in nature were only a few hours away. Coming upon the Sepulveda pass Dave heard sirens in the distance and noticed red flashing lights in his rear view mirror. There seemed to be a police pursuit and the pursued car was driving recklessly fast, weaving in and out of traffic at dangerous speeds. As the car made hazardous, quick lane changes, it clipped Dave's rear bumper causing him to fish tail; hitting two cars, flipping over and landing bottom side up while sliding horizontally across the freeway lanes. Tires of other cars could be heard screeching as brakes are applied. Smoke emission was coming from the tires of an 18-wheeler Peterbilt Semi-trailer truck as the driver brakes trying to avoid hitting Dave's car, but he broadsides him on the driver's side.

There was pandemonium as the freeway was brought to a halt; completely shut down. The pursued driver and the two passengers in the car were allegedly involved in an armed robbery and shooting. With the exception of a few scrapes and cuts they were treated at the scene and carted off to jail facing a host of charges including attempted robbery, aggravated assault and possible manslaughter.

Paramedics and the fire department quickly arrive on scene and the vehicle is so mangled they use the "jaws of life" to extricate Dave from the rumpled pile. Fitted with a neck brace and placed on a backboard they use defibrillator paddles to jump start his heart twice, his lifeless body jolted and flopped from the electrical charge before getting a pulse. As he's stabilized Dave is loaded into an ambulance and transported to the nearest hospital. Paramedics radio ahead so the emergency room could be prepared to attend to his massive injuries upon arrival. Dave was in critical condition.

The radio message was; "...55-60 aged male, massive head trauma and internal bleeding; eyes are fixed and dilated and pulse is 60/40."

In the emergency room on the treatment table Dave's heart stopped again and the defibrillator was used but his injuries are too invasive for the medical team to save him. As the emergency room doctor calls the time of death, Dave's spirit was floating above his body. He looked down on the table and saw his shell was a bloody, marred mess. Off in the distance a bright light was drawing him as two celestial beings hovered on each side of that light. Undoubtedly, they are Angels, indescribable majestic Beings. As he is drawn nearer to the light, he recognizes other spirits waiting there to meet him. He saw family, friends and loved ones all illuminating life but not as we know it. There was also a melodious sound comparable to that of music but yet an inexpressible euphonious sound he'd never known and had nothing to compare it too. As family was notified the emergency room team cleaned his body and prepared him for delivery to the hospital morgue.

Dave had been a Christian for one year and he was going to the mountains with his sister and her family. He spent a lot of time with them since he stopped his binge drinking. Dave's wife and children were killed in a crosswalk, one block from their home by a drunk driver while walking home from school. The driver plowed through the crosswalk at a horrendous speed, killing them instantly. The impact spewed their bodies into the air landing them sprawled and disfigured in the busy intersection.

After months of grieving and continuous binge drinking Dave found a note written by his wife in her bible. The note read, "God, please save my husband." He struggled to hold back tears as he clutched the bible to his chest.

Attending bible study and listening to the end of a teaching series on heaven, Dave knew heaven was where he wanted to spend his eternity. This was the final night of the teaching and Dave accepted Christ as his Savior. For a year after the tragic death of his family (wife and three small children), Dave walked with and lived for God.

He beat all odds and was clean and sober from alcohol addiction. He declared himself free from a generational curse of superstition and witchcraft. His survival of the murder of his mother at the hands of his father and the tragic death of his entire family was incredible. Now he too would live the promise of God, eternal life in…heaven.

ABOUT THE AUTHOR
Shiela Y. Harris

As a retiree Shiela spends the majority of her time writing, seeing to the needs of her 92 year old mother, working in ministry and volunteering in community service.

Born in the 50's; a baby boomer, living to see the 21st century unfold she has learned the importance of fully sequestering life. She enjoys nature, life in the city and enjoys friends and family. It is also important to her that she honors God with her life.

For each added birthday experienced she feels blessed in so many ways. Life to her is everyday school because she is always vigorously tapping into academia, absorbing and gaining knowledge and continues to nourish her mind, intellect and emotions.

> Trust in the Lord with all thine heart; and lean not unto thine own understanding. In all thy ways acknowledge Him, and He shall direct they paths. Proverbs 3:5-6